· PREPOSTEROUS ·

LIBRIS

ex LIBRIS

· FABLES ·

PREPOSTEROUS FABLES FOR UNUSUAL CHILDREN

The Tooth Fairy

The Maestro

The Wolf King

The Sorcerer's Last Words

The Giant Killer

THE GIANT KILLER

Written and illustrated
by Judd Palmer

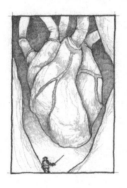

BAYEUX

Special Thanks: Marilyn Palmer, Steve Pearce, Jill Boettger,
Renée Amber, Jim Palmer, Dave Lane, Jenny Lane, the Trouts,
Ashis Gupta.

THE GIANT KILLER
© 2004 Judd Palmer and Bayeux Arts, Inc.
Published by: Bayeux Arts, Inc., 119 Stratton Crescent SW, Calgary,
Canada T3H 1T7 www.bayeux.com

Cover design by David Lane & Judd Palmer
Typography and book design by David Lane
Edited by Jennifer Mattern

Library and Archives Canada Cataloguing in Publication
Palmer, Judd, 1972-
   The giant killer / written and illustrated by Judd Palmer.
   (Preposterous fables for unusual children ; no. 5)
   ISBN 1-896209-47-5
  Title. II. Series: Palmer, Judd, 1972- Preposterous fables
  for unusual children; no. 5.

PS8581.A555G52 2004 jC813'.6 C2004-905692-1

First Printing: November 2004
Printed in Canada

The Publisher gratefully acknowledges the financial support of the Canada
Council for the Arts, the Alberta Foundation for the Arts, and the Government
of Canada through The Book Publishing Industry Development Program.

for Tim

Saint George the Great Dragon did slay,

Hunters wild boars make compliant,

And beasts of the forests way-lay;

Jack is the dread of the Giant.

Pray who has not heard of his fame?

His actions so bold and unpliant;

The friend of the rich and the poor,

But never afraid of the giant.

—J.G. Rusher, *The History of Jack
the Giant Killer*, 1820

"And so too end the memoirs of Jack, known as the Giant Killer."

Chapter One

LO! WITH A MIGHTY storm-roar, the Last of the Giants swung his iron mountain-masher around his hoary head. Through the icy air it circled hurtling, swirling the mists like a great spoon in a soup made of clouds, and I, Jack the Giant Killer, saw the deadly blow that the Giant plotted. Astride my trusted battle steed, the Golden Hen of legend, I shouted my noble defiance: "You shall plague humanity no more, and neither shall your kind, for you are the Last of the Giants. You have lived to see the end of your times, but you shall not live to see the dawning of this next day, the bright dawning of the world unshackled, the happy rising of the sun upon the earth, upon which your foot-prints shall fade and then be forgotten. With your last breath shall evil also be exhaled from the universe, like a lungful of fetid swamp-fog, and it shall be Jack the Giant Killer who stands triumphant on your mountainous corpse."

The Last of the Giants brought his crushing cudgel down with a shriek that tore the sky, meaning to make a paste of me. Nimble-leaping upon my steed I dodged that terrible blow. A small village full of gentle people, plus a swath of forest containing a herd of innocent deer and a community of kindly rabbits, paid the price the Giant meant for me to pay. I saw with righteous rage that the Giant had caused yet more misery, and vowed aloud that it would be the last visitation of sorrow the race of Giants would bring to the world. As I vowed it, I raced to attack bravely, the Golden Hen flapping courageously to fling me into the air.

CHAPTER ONE

I raised my gauntletted fist, which gripped my famous sword, CloudSlicer, and struck the Last of the Giants a heroic blow in the pupil of his left eye. The Giant issued a cry of torment that caused a flock of geese fifty miles away to be blown off course, and while distracted by this pain he did not properly guard his nostrils, for which I flew immediately. Up the Giant's nose I went, whilst the Giant flailed. I was buffeted by the Giant's desperate sneezing, but nobly I forged on, for no sneeze could dislodge a hero so pure of heart. To the Giant's tender brain I clambered, and there smote with CloudSlicer the mortal blow to the Last of the Giants, whose bellowing stopped upon the instant the sword found its mark in his mind. The Giant heard my voice inside his head as he toppled, and these were the final words heard by the final Giant upon the Earth:

"So now is your end, and it was Jack that brought it. You may have been big, but you should have been good, like Jack, whose goodness is as famous as your evil was bad. Look upon the world *which you are leaving, and know that it will be happier in your absence. Give thought to that, as your lights dim, and know that such shall not be the last thoughts of Jack, who will always know that the world bears him great gratitude, for Jack is the saviour of his kind. He is the light, whereas you are the dark; all love him—for he is Jack the Giant Killer."*

And so the Last of the Giants repented as his kind disappeared forever from the Earth.

Jack ponders a moment, and then adds a final rueful line:

And so too end the memoirs of Jack, known as the Giant Killer, for there were no more deeds to do. All that could be done was done, and that was the end of it.

Jack stares at the period at the end of the sentence he has just written. It seems to stare back at him, like the pupil of a dread eye.

The Last of the Giants died seventy years ago. Three generations have passed since last their mighty feet trod and shook this earth, and

CHAPTER ONE

most of those who have ever seen a Giant are now dead themselves. But Jack lives on, growing smaller and smaller each day as his body shrivels and wrinkles, as his bones grow brittle and his bladder disobedient. He sits at his desk like a crumpled wad of paper, propped up with pillows, his dry fingers clutching his quill with white knuckles to keep from trembling.

He sits back in his chair, his bony bum creaking as he shifts. He blinks. Who gives a ferret's fart, he thinks, if I lie a little? They're my memoirs, and I can remember whatever I like.

Chapter Two

THE SUN, NEWLY RISEN, comes through the window. Jack looks for all the world like a dust-mote, so ethereally ancient is he; he is still sitting at his desk with the completed memoirs before him. He is dressed in his night cap and pajamas, a kerchief tied around his jaw to soothe a toothache. The sunlight catches the ridges and furrow-peaks of his wrinkled head. He is fidgeting with the quill. He is not yet quite ready to put it down.

The sun continues to fill the room slowly.

In the pale growing glimmer certain details become visible: the ink well, the bits of ripped paper scattered about (failed final chapters), the fallen bottle of wine, the wine itself, now a sticky pool that reaches across the desk like a crimson archipelago. Behind him, his sword upon a stand. A curious helmet beside it, a cape embroidered with strange patterns, tall black boots. Beyond, an abandoned sandwich. A door.

The papers rustle gently as the door opens. Jack looks up with grey eyes.

"Ah, good morning, my delightful-most dear," he says. "And how is my little toad-spittle today?"

Amelia, his wife, is peering in. "Just grand, my dearest husband. Purest joy, of course, to see you again today as yesterday and the day before that and so on. You are as constant as my arthritis, my love. As dependable as flatulence after broccoli. As inescapable as the gaping mouths of graveyard worms. I see you are still ruminating upon your memoirs."

"Indeed I am, my beloved buttock-boil. I see you are just getting up, looking forward, no doubt, to another day of useless breathing."

"Yes, indeed. Just as the fairy-tales tell it, I always think: happily ever after. That's us. Well, I mustn't keep you from your important efforts at literature. The world would never forgive me if I delayed you, even for a moment, in case that moment proved to have been crucial to the completion of your masterpiece before you expire."

Amelia's head disappeared back into the hall.

"I'm finished," said Jack, to no-one in particular, or no-one who cared, at any rate.

He looked upon the most beautiful girl he had ever seen.

Chapter Three

WITH GALIGANTUS DEAD, and the evil Sorcerer chased away for good, the spell over the castle was broken. Like a newborn taking its first breath, the castle filled with life: courtiers' cheeks flushed once more, servants awoke surprised with feast platters still in their hands, musicians finished plucking the notes they had begun so many years before. The Duke himself opened his eyes on his throne and looked about. The tear that had sprung from his eye on the day the spell was cast finished its passage to his beard, only now it was a tear of joy, not misery, transformed as it passed over his cheek.

I stood in wonder as the castle came to life around me, and the darkness slithered away like its master. I was so young, yet so heroic already—for it was I, Jack the Giant Killer, who had saved the people from their cruel imprisonment.

I looked upon what I had wrought, and spied the most beautiful girl I had ever seen, still frozen upon the throne next to her father the Duke. She was like a shimmering icicle, so perfect in her stillness, her slender neck long and elegant, her lips full and red and slightly parted. And then, glorious glorious, her breast heaved once more. Her eyelashes fluttered. She raised her gentle eyes, and looked around her in amazement, and what she saw was me. She smiled.

"You have saved us from the evil spell of the Sorcerer," said the Duke. "What is your name, young man?"

"Jack," said I, "the Giant Killer."

CHAPTER THREE

"*Jack the Giant Killer*," said the Duke. "*I am so very grateful. I hope you will marry my beautiful daughter.*"

And I did, and we lived happily ever after.

Jack grimaces, reading that passage. Amelia was the first princess he ever saved. But she certainly wasn't the last. That has been a bit of a problem with his marriage.

A gathering is happening in those murks.

Chapter Four

BEYOND THIS WORLD is a land of ice. It is colder there than ghosts' bones, and as far as can be seen it is boundless white. It is so immense that it seems unmoving, the land of ice, but in fact the frozen ground is in constant uproar, slow as the moon but as implacable, great islands of ice grinding against each other, their shores in a turmoil of pressure, cracking and heaving. It is a landscape of eternal war.

One island will conquer the shores of another, and the vanquished will break into scattered refugee pieces that groan and scrape on the underside of the victor. Below the islands is the cold sea, dark, depthless, shifting silently. A gathering is happening in those murks: the ancient tribes of the Cod of the North are coming, for something is happening in the darkness.

Like clammy phantoms the legions of fish slip through the swelling tides, from faraway, at the call of the Cod King. They pack together in expectant rows, their cold bodies pressed one to another, their eyes fixed above on the ice-roof that is the sky of their domain. Their slimy brains are full of wonder, for a mystical event foretold by their forefathers is about to occur. The frozen vault of heaven is about to be torn asunder, and a god released.

For the greatest iceberg battle in history is taking place. Two mountains grapple above the coddish audience. It has taken ten thousand years for these greatest of their kind to come together in war, so ponderous is their progress, and the first impact of their clashing charge itself happened before the Cod King was born. For lifetimes they have wrestled, their vast weights straining and pressing, and now the cod are gathered to see the final victory of one over the other.

With a groan and shriek so slow it sounds as if the moon is crashing to earth, the Coddish heaven erupts downwards into the deep. The conquered berg breaks in two, an explosion made of cold. The whole of the North shudders, and the fish are hurled against the ocean floor a mile below the thundering surface. They struggle back, dazed, to see what the death of an iceberg has wrought.

Now there is only one nameless Emperor of the Ice. All the icebergs of the North bob and tip in homage, and the vanquished contender, torn asunder, begins its ten-thousand-year retreat. It is a mountain sheared: ice born beyond time is exposed to the world it has not seen for millennia.

But there is something else. Something protruding from the innards of the beaten one. Something that looks like a hand, only so very much bigger. It is frozen white, the colour of the Cod King's belly.

Its fingers twitch. Its owner has awoken. The cod rejoice.

Chapter Five

ON JACK'S DESK is his quill. Beside it is the closed book of his memoirs. A flame flickers in a pool of wax that once was a candle. Jack is gone.

Let us trace his trudges from this place. From the desk to the rack behind it, to don his helmet and cape and boots and clutch his sword with fingers trembling like dead branches in the wind. A sigh, and then over to the door, opened then passed through. From here we can see that he has made his home in a castle once owned by a Giant; his study is in a cupboard. On a shelf nearby, the chambers of Amelia, in a kettle with copper walls. A bridge has been built between the two, made of iron and rusted now.

Below the bridge the Kitchen sprawls. In the distance, a stove, a cutting block once used by the Giant to dismember the ingredients for his stew, now a disused tennis court. The kitchen table is still littered with the remains of a party Jack and Amelia had twenty years ago, when they still had visitors—empty bottles, decomposing decorations, a single shoe abandoned on the dance floor.

A long staircase leads from the cupboard to the flagstones below. Between the flagstones, a hallway lined with paintings of flowers—a passion of Amelia's thirty years ago—now grimy. In the dust, the footprints of Jack can be seen in faltering progress towards his destination.

Is there a fork in the path, a hall leading to the children's rooms? Empty now, but lovingly kept tidy for when they come home for Christmas? There is not. This hall is straight and unwavering. Once, the idea of children came up, when Amelia and Jack were toying temporarily with the idea of immortality through progeny. The conversation turned to possible names; Amelia favoured 'Sophia' if a girl, and 'Edward' if a boy. If it turned out to be a boy, Jack favoured 'Jack,' and if a girl, 'Jack.' The conversation grew intractable, and now the hallway has no other directions.

The hall goes only one direction, to the Hall of Trophies. Jack's trail leads there.

A vast room, walls shadowed and distant. Assembled for viewing are the trophies Jack has gathered over his life, each as enormous as its former owner, displayed upon decrepit oceans of red velvet upon pedestals with plaques that once described the object they support. Here, a battered brass helmet, which could be identified as the battle-crown of Olaf Stonebeard the Enormous, if the plaque was not illegibly green with patina. Here, the jeweled gauntlets of Cormorant, late of St. Michael's Mount. There, the matching nose-rings of Old Blunderbore and his brother. Over there, the club of Ods Splutter Hur Nails, the codpiece of Uncle Threeheads, the severed beard of Thundel (and the moustaches of his younger brothers). The Golden Harp from the cloud-palace of the very first Giant Jack slayed, its strings trembling in a mournful minor chord as if shivered by the fingers of a breeze, although the air is still and heavy. The instrument that gave its name once to Galligantus of the Trumpet, whose last note was blown by Jack to break the spell that froze the Duke and his court. All asleep beneath a blanket of dust, a strange geography of grey powder, a world of it, waist deep. A furrow marking the passage of

Jack not long ago, now settling back like a wound closing.

And there is Jack. He sits atop a mound of golden eggs. He is clad in his war-regalia: the Helmet of Knowledge, the Cape of Invisibility, the Boots of Swiftness, his sword, CloudSlicer, across his bony knees. He sighs, and waits for the end.

Far away, Amelia is asleep in her kettle, and the candle on Jack's desk sputters out.

Chapter Six

THE WIND BLOWS ACROSS the Northern wastes, picking up gusts of stinging snowflakes. The heavens are bright with stars above, and the moon casts a phantom blue glimmer onto the jagged white landscape. The ice-crag shadows are long, grasping fingers of darkness. The only sound is the wind's whisper and moan.

Far off, a new sound, strange to this frozen sea. It is part bellow, part volcano-roar. The snow squalls swirl like panicking ghosts. What staggers through the dread emptiness? What bellows in the blue night?

The stars blink out, forming an impossible silhouette. Too huge a thing is blocking the moon; a shadow stretches across the ice like an entirely new night has been invented.

There in the moonlight, a glimpse of white flesh, an ear? A hoary temple, a frost-rimed nose? Another bellow that makes the ice groan and crackle.

A Giant has been released from the vanquished iceberg. The Last Giant was not the last Giant. This, now, in the arctic void, is the Very Last Giant, stretching his vast limbs in the cold moonlight, unfrozen now for the first time in ten thousand years.

He cannot remember how he came to be locked in an iceberg. All he knows is that now he is free. He bellows again, to feel the air in his lungs, to hear his voice echo in the vault of heaven, to know he is alive. It is a bellow of joy.

He stomps his feet and waves his arms. He twirls on one toe. The Giant is dancing.

Chapter Seven

SOMETIMES AMELIA REMEMBERS her life before Jack, her life as a princess. It was wonderful to be a beautiful princess, but there was a plague upon her kingdom.

Looking back, she realizes it wasn't exactly the plague they thought it was. A Giant had moved in nearby, and everybody thought the Giant was the problem, but the sad truth of it was, the Giant never bothered anybody, until they decided to send a knight to kill it.

Amelia had liked the knight. He used to make up poems to charm her, and he could sort of play the harp. Mostly she liked the fact that he liked her so much, but that's really all a princess needs, after all.

So she had been teary-eyed when he set forth on his horse to kill the Giant. She gave him her handkerchief as a token; later she thought she should have come up with something more meaningful, but he waved it at her in his gauntletted hand like it was the best gift in the world as he rode out the gates. He never came back.

Amelia pretended to mourn, but there was another young man who caught her eye quite soon after. He was quite dashing when he boldly proclaimed he would kill the Giant. Of course, he didn't come back either.

Nor did the next one, or the next, or the next, and in this way the plague settled upon the kingdom—a plague that took only brave young boys. And after a while, it took boys that weren't so brave.

CHAPTER SEVEN

And then, one day, the Giant came to the castle. Amelia was staggered by the size of him, she remembers. Her heart was filled with wonder and terror combined. All the remaining men, mostly old or weak, made a big show of grabbing their weapons and shaking them, but they all saw why none of the boys had come back. The Giant could smash the entire castle with one blow.

The Giant spoke to them. "Why can't you people leave me alone?" he asked. Everybody yelled their battle-yells and tried to poke his toes with their spears.

So the Giant left, shaking his head. Amelia lay in her bed that night, unable to sleep, the sounds of the old men getting drunk and bragging about the day's bravery down the hall. She had never seen something so large. She had never realized how big the universe could be, how very much bigger than her little throne surrounded by tiny crooning boys.

The Giant returned the next day, accompanied by a strange man in a black travelling cloak.

Everybody got out their weapons again and did their bravery thing. The Giant spoke to the mysterious stranger.

"Give them peace," he said. "I don't want them to suffer. I just want them to calm down."

The man in the cloak nodded, and waved his hands. He began to whisper.

What's the point of all this bluster? Why get so worked up? Nobody's convinced. We can all see through it. It's all for show; life's nothing but a show—full of sound and fury, as they say, signifying nothing. There is no point.

The Sorcerer's whispers blew like a gentle breeze through the castle, through the doors and windows and cracks in the walls, into ears and around brains and into hearts. Slowly, slowly, everybody stopped yelling. Slowly, slowly, everybody stopped caring. Slowly,

slowly, everybody settled into what felt like a really nice nap on a Sunday afternoon.

They wouldn't wake up from that nap for forty years, until Jack the Giant Killer came and broke the spell.

But Amelia still very much liked to have a nap on a Sunday afternoon. More often, if possible.

Amelia awakes in her bed, and looks at the clock. The thing ticks slowly, and she watches its hands for awhile, willing them to move only just a little faster, calculating the hours that she must be awake before she can sleep again. The day lies before her like a desert trek or a doldrum sea; she is small as a bird but her old bones feel heavy as boulders.

She has never quite shaken the Sorcerer's enchantment. Her life in the castle of her youth, paralyzed by magic, eyes unblinking and seeing nothing, still lurks in the pit of her. The possibility for total stillness has always gnawed at her, and now in her age she does not have the strength to combat it. She lifts her arm but the Sorcerer's whisper convinces her to drop it again. *What are you going to do with that arm? Nothing of any consequence. Put it down.*

She watches her chest rise and fall, listens to the soft rasp of her lungs, secretly gathering her strength to sit up. She must do it suddenly and decisively, to surprise the ghost of the Sorcerer inside, catch him off guard so that he doesn't have a chance to talk her out of it.

Victory! She is sitting up. She can hear the dread whispering inside, *lie back down, get back under the covers*, but now she has momentum, she is standing in her nightgown and putting on her slippers and shuffling away from her bed. She's not sure what she wants to do, but she can't think of that now. She ought to brush her hair, but then she'll be tempted to sit down, and she has to keep moving. Her hand reaches

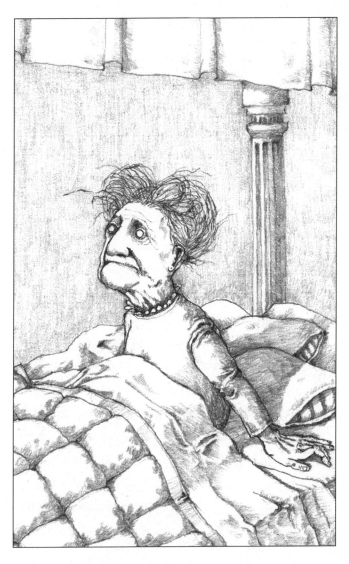

She can hear the dread whispering inside.

the door. She turns the handle. She is out of her bedroom. The Sorcerer is at bay, for the moment.

There is nothing to do, of course. There hasn't been anything to do for her entire life, as the wife of the Giant Killer. Except: hold onto what she is. Envy and destroy all that threatens. Keep Jack at all costs. For this task her will is strong, but even her will is thus turned towards stillness of a sort.

She has always known that a different, opposite sorcerer whispers inside Jack. It says to him: *There is a bigger Giant yet to slay.* It says: *Jack the Giant Killer Jack the Giant Killer Jack the Giant Killer.*

And where is Jack now? She glances about. She can sense he is not in his study; she is subtly tuned this way, after many years of practice. She will find him. She has a purpose, for today, at least.

Chapter Eight

JACK SITS, WAITING TO DIE, on a pile of golden eggs. Amelia wanders the vast ramparts slowly, wheezing, searching for him.

Far away they hear a knock at the gates. For a moment they are connected by it, as their heads swivel on their wrinkled necks towards the bizarre sound. A visitor. The first in decades.

They are frozen, each in their places, Amelia and Jack, their hard-won purposes threatened. Another knock.

Both wrench themselves into action. Amelia scampers in her slippers towards her bedroom to get dressed. It will not do to greet a visitor in her nightgown. Jack takes a deep rattling breath and heaves himself to his feet. There is a loud creak, and for a moment Jack thinks the visitor must have swung open the rusty-hinged gate. Then he realizes it was his knees that made the noise as he stood. He creaks, tottering, down into the sea of dust. He wades through it with a growing excitement.

Another knock.

In the entrance hall they see each other. They are each in their regalia, although Amelia's hair-brushing has been unsuccessful in her unaccustomed haste, and Jack is a cloud of dust. They look as if they have risen from their graves to greet their guest, and each thinks the other is an embarrassment. They are too confused and excited to think of any insults, so they turn towards the door and straighten themselves for the impact of the mysterious visitor.

Together they open the gate, holding their breath. And there before them is the visitor. *Two* visitors.

One of them bellows. "By me barnacled bum! Are ye ghosts?"

He is a lump. He has no arms or legs, and sits egglike in a wheelchair. He has a bristling beard, so wiry and grey it could be used to scrub a pot. He is missing his two front teeth, and he is wearing a crown, studded with strange teeth. His eyes are alight with terror, and he writhes in his seat like a grub.

Behind him is a large fellow with a simple dullness in his features, a face like a pile of rocks. He wears an oily top hat and has large hands rough as old oars, gripping the back of the wheelchair. He utters a strange groan of fear.

"Not yet ghosts," says Jack, peering confused at the pair.

"By me barnacled bum! Are ye ghosts?"

"Hardly ghosts," sniffs Amelia, offended.

"Are ye Jack the Giant Killer, then?" says the bristling wad.

Jack tries to stifle a grin of joy. "I am," he says heroically.

"And ye live and breathe?"

"Indeed I do, always at the ready."

"Well, then, allow me to introduce meself," says the stump. "Ye will have heard of me no doubt. I am Captain Bleak, the Whaler-King. This is me first mate, Stoat. Come from the North, we have. There be a Giant there."

Chapter Nine

THE FOUR ARE SITTING in Jack's study.

"Aye, a Giant," says Bleak. "Each leg as big as a Humpback Fishy on end with its wife and kids stacked on top. Nobody knows where it come from. Crashing about, it is, wreaking havoc 'mongst the Siberians."

'A terrible thing, a Giant," agrees Jack. "Yes, an evil, evil thing, a scourge upon us good people. I must gather my weapons and set forth at once."

"Aye, at once. I have a ship, I do. Fast as a leopard if a leopard was fast on the sea, me ship. What have ye got to muster up, weapons-wise?"

"I have my famous Helmet of Knowledge, which answers any question; I have my magic Cape which makes me invisible when I wish it. I have my Boots of Swiftness, and my noble sword, CloudSlicer, which cuts anything it touches. I must only gather my Golden Hen and we shall be off."

"My, that Giant don't stand a chance, do he? All that stuff." Bleak nods his head, grinning. He twists around and winks at Stoat. "A power of stuff, arr, eh Stoat?" he says. Stoat grunts, a big stupid smile on his face.

"Indeed, a deadly array. Each enchanted weapon liberated from the clutches of a foul Giant. Each has done noble service for me in bygone years, as I in turn have done humble service to humanity with their help. It has been a hard life, sir; many a time people have said to me, 'Jack, you've done enough, why don't you rest?' I have always stalwartly said: 'Nay.' 'Nay,' I've said, 'not while the Giant kind still rampages can I rest.'"

Jack is getting worked up. "'Nay! Nay! Nay, and three times more, nay,' I say. For the suffering of humanity is my suffering. The suffering of the Siberians, why, I feel it too, in my heart, which aches for them! And while I still breathe, while strength still lingers in my fingers and toes, I must do what I can to make the world a better place! For I am Jack! Jack the Giant Killer! I cannot rest!"

Jack slumps back in his chair, exhausted. Bleak and Stoat nod at him, impressed. Amelia frowns.

Jack turns to her. "My beloved, I'll need some clean underwear. And a towel. Be a dear, and pack up my suitcase." He turns back to Bleak as Amelia stands up. He doesn't notice the expression on her face as she leaves the room.

Jack hears the door close behind her, and then leans forward conspiratorially. "Captain Bleeb," he whispers, "I must ask—"

"Bleak. It's Captain Bleak."

"Ah, yes, terribly sorry. Bleak. Captain Bleak, sir, I must ask: do you happen to know, are there any princesses at risk?"

Bleak nods. "Oh, aye, there is indeed," he whispers. "A Siberian Princess, famous for her beauty, aye. Dressed always in white fur, she is, with red lips so lovely sailors say they are as deadly as a harpoon. Poor dear thing," he adds, winking, "nobody can save her from the dread Giant in that land."

Jack stifles a grin, trying to look as if the very thought breaks his heart. He leans back in his chair and then realizes Amelia has returned.

"Just going over the battle plan, my dearest," he says. "Much too complicated for your pretty brain to grasp."

He looks up, and to his confusion, she is

wearing a heavy parka and holding a rucksack. She fixes him with a terrifying stare.

"I'm coming along, dearest."

Jack gurgles in surprise. He knows that stare, and he knows he stands no chance against it, even with all his wondrous weapons. "Oh," he stammers, "wonderful. What a rare delight! You've never accompanied me on my missions before, dear. How much more confident I shall be knowing you are waiting on the ship whilst I fight the Giant!"

"Let's be off, then," says Amelia, who has heard every secret word on the subject of princesses from behind the door. In truth, she hadn't needed to eavesdrop. She knows Jack's every deceitful thought by now; the Sorcerer inside her whispers the details of every betrayal. Age has honed her into a knife with one purpose. This time she will not allow Jack his princess.

Of course, something far worse than a storm is coming.

Chapter Ten

IN A JUNGLE CITY IN HINDUSTAN, a man
is singing a song to a girl he hopes will love
him; he feels a small pinprick on his arm, slaps
at it, and squashes a mosquito famous amongst
mosquitoes for her beautiful legs. On a grassy
plain near Moose Jaw, an ant genius is about to
realize a mathematical equation that will
change utterly the destiny of ants, someday
making them the rulers of the world, when a
woman puts her lunch down on top of him,
and he is crushed by the cruel weight of a vast

salami. In the bottom of a coffee cup some-where in France (nobody will remember pre-cisely where), a bit of mold is about to write a masterpiece of mold poetry when a certain Jean-Jacques LaFontaine, automobile mechanic, washes his cup, erasing that poem from future memory forever. In Siberia, a man named Yevgeny Piotrarovitch wearing a fur hat is thinking nothing in particular (except that per-haps a stroll might be nice this afternoon) when an unexpected foot from the sky ruins his afternoon plans entirely.

The Giant doesn't notice. He lifts his foot again and puts it down a mile away from Yevgeny Piotrarovitch. Even if the Giant had been watching his feet, he wouldn't have seen Yevgeny Piotrarovitch, because the Giant's head is poking through the clouds and he can't see the ground. From above the clouds, it appears as if his head is a ship on a foggy sea, his nose the prow, his eyes portholes, his hair some strange variety of tangled sails, his grinning mouth the tooth-planked hull. He is humming a tune that he's making up, a song tentatively titled 'How Wonderful It Is to Be Alive.' It's a lively little jig that would sound good on a violin or an accordion, but hummed by the Giant it is so loud that people below think a terrible storm is coming.

Of course, something far worse than a storm is coming. A Giant is on his way, with his head floating on the clouds and his feet smashing new valleys into the earth below. But the Giant doesn't know that he brings disaster to the little people.

The Giant doesn't know either that another ship is approaching—a ship on the sea, not a ship on the clouds. He does not see the ragged sails, or hear the hoarse cries of the sailors on the shrouds, the crack and snap of the mizzen-lines, and the black flag flutter of the Whaler King. He doesn't see the tiny figures arranged

on the poop deck: the hairy clump in his wheelchair, the silent trollish wheelchair-pusher, the
wizened old woman in the parka with the
Sorcerer in her heart, and the ancient bonebag
festooned with the regalia of war, all rustled by
the sea-wind. He doesn't know their thoughts;
he doesn't know they are coming to kill him.

He pauses for a moment to scratch his
armpit, and it feels so good, he decides to
scratch his chest as well. He giggles at how
wonderful it is to scratch an itch. He is looking
forward to being itchy again, so that he will be
able to scratch himself once more. A new line
of his song occurs to him, and he bellows it
joyously.

Chapter Eleven

THE WHALING SHIP SURGES through dark waves. It is getting colder, and icebergs can be seen off the prow in the distance. Frost is gathering on the rigging. Jack is below decks, tending to the Golden Hen, brushing her feathers, polishing her beak, scrubbing her wattle. She clucks appreciatively. He is thinking about red lips when the door opens and Stoat maneuvers Captain Bleak into the room. Stoat stares bluntly at the wall.

"I hope ye don't mind a visit, Jack," says Bleak. "A wee sip of rum, for ye, arr?"

"Why, certainly, Captain Gleak," says Jack, obligingly, putting down his wattle-scrubber.

Bleak winces but then grins. "So this be the Golden Hen, aye? The Lustrous Chicken, of sailor's yarns, what I heard of in salty taverns and in hushed-hushed wink-winks under the fo'c'sle planks at night? Arr?"

"The Golden Hen, indeed, Captain Blear," says Jack, taking a tin cup of rum from Stoat. "She is my most trusted steed, and she lays eggs of gold, to boot."

Bleak slurps at a cup tipped to his chapped lips by his rock-like first mate. "I've often thought, I have, that we have a common way, ye and I," he says. "Ye be a killer of Giants on two feet, arr, whereas I be a killer of those with flukes and spouts, aye. Both of us Giant killers, y'see." Bleak peers at Jack with one eye scrunched.

"I see," says Jack. "I suppose there's a similarity, in a way."

"Aye, a similarity, as ye say. A funny thing, though. Landlubbers don't see it. Poor old Captain Bleak, me, he comes home to port from a-whalin', and no crowds 'pon the docks a-cheerin' and what-not. No princess for old Bleak, y'see. No pretty eggs of gold for me. No huzzah. Not right, I say."

"I see your point, Captain Dweek."

Bleak wriggles a little closer to Jack. "Aye, my point, ye see it. Arr. Do I not live a life of danger 'pon the high seas? Did I suffer, or not?"

"I am sure you have suffered in your escapades, sir."

"Do ye see any arms and legs upon me, Jack? Do ye?"

Jack isn't sure what to say. Bleak is getting a little frothy for his liking. "I hadn't noticed before, but now that you mention it, sir, I do not."

"Ten years spent I in the innards of a whale, Jack. Put there by the guiles of a wee girl wit' pretty teeth, curse her soul. Uncommon cold in there, the whale's guts, did ye know that? Froze me legs right off o' me bum, just dropped right off, none but buttocks to hold me up now, and them's shriveled right up too. A cruel fate, but who cares about it?"

Jack tries hard not to picture Bleak's bum.

"And me arms, lost 'em to the effects of gastric juices, didn't I? That whale digested 'em right off me. If it waren't for a grueling effort to find his sphincter in the dark, who knows what kind of man might sit before ye today? Nothin' but a head!"

For some reason this notion makes Bleak chortle weirdly, sputtering and barking. Jack realizes that the man is stark mad.

Suddenly Bleak is not laughing anymore. "But when I come a-bobbin' back to port, do they cry 'Huzzah, it's Bleak, the Giant Killer?'"

"Well, to be honest, I'm the Giant Killer," mutters Jack.

"I killt more Giants than ye! I killt a hundred hundred of 'em, and scraped 'em and boiled 'em and made 'em into buckets of oil! And paid the cost! Tell me whales ain't big, Jack. Tell me they ain't Giants, and I'll tell ye, fine, if they ain't big, then I ain't a Giant Killer."

"Whales are big, you're right."

"There ye be, then," grunts the raving lump. "Giant Killer, me."

"Whales are innocent, however," says Jack.

"Innocent!" Bleak shrieks. "Innocent!" he boils. "Did I sprout legs and arms before ye? Am I not dismasted? Am I not a sorry chunk? Was it an innocent beasty that made me such a sausage?" He flops about in his chair so furiously that Stoat must hold him down.

Jack thinks the argument may be too complicated to make headway. He gives up. "You are right, Captain Fweet. You are absolutely right."

"Captain Bleak!" froths Bleak. "Get it right, Jack. Captain Bleak, me. Captain Bleak, the Giant Killer!"

Chapter Twelve

JACK IS FEELING considerably beleaguered. Bleak has called a council of war, and Jack, despite having no intention of involving the whaler in his plans, feels it may be safest to attend. And to make matters worse, Amelia has also insisted on being present.

They are sitting around Bleak's dinner table. Bleak presides from his wheelchair, lashed to the floor so that it won't roll with the ship's pitch and yaw. Stoat handles a fork and knife with surprising delicacy, carving a bit of fried blubber and maneuvering it to Bleak's mouth, pausing for him to rant, waiting for the right moment to slip the bite in between ravings. Jack sits uncomfortably with Amelia glowering at his side.

"Right," says Bleak, "here's wot I proposes, me. We sails right up to the Giant, y' see, and then I cries 'all hands' like I do, and we chase the monster in rowboats with harpoons. We stick 'im, y' see, with the harpoons, until he rolls under, spouting black blood, and there she be, dead Giant."

Bleak sits back and munches, satisfied.

Jack looks at his fork. "It won't work."

Bleak farts in alarm. "Why not?"

"He'll smash your boats, and your harpoons will be pinpricks to him. We must be more clever than that. Using my Helmet of Knowledge, I have devised a perfect plan."

"Let's 'ear it, then, Jack, don't keep us waitin'."

"I fly towards him on my faithful steed,

using my Cape of Invisibility, so that he cannot
see me approach. Then, I land on his head.
Thereby I gain the advantage—although he
will be able to feel my feet on his skin, I will use
my Boots of Swiftness to rapidly maneuver out
of the way of his fists. Nevertheless, he will
attempt to smash me, but in continually missing he will beat himself about the skull until he
is sufficiently beleaguered by his own efforts
for me to make my way into his ear. Nobly, I
will clamber inside his head where he cannot
reach me at all. Then, using my famous sword,
CloudSlicer, I can dispose of his brain at my
leisure. It is a variation on a method I perfected
wherein I fly up the Giant's nose. It has not
failed yet."

Bleak grunts menacingly. "Wot do I do?"

Jack winces to himself. "The one flaw in my
plan: the Giant's famous capacity for smelling.
He must be distracted from my odour. That, my
good friend, is where you come in, for you are a

powerfully smelly thing. You will fill the air with your fragrance, concealing me therefore from the Giant's detection."

Bleak growls.

"Without you, Captain Bleak, the plan will never work."

Bleak squints.

"The whole world will thank you for your crucial role."

Bleak twitches.

"They will say, thank heavens for Bleak, noble Bleak, He Who Was So Very Instrumental In The Death Of That Evil Giant."

Bleak grins. "Bleak the Giant Killer, ye mean to say?"

Bleak looks like a ferocious potato. Jack acquiesces. "Yes. That's right. Bleak the Giant Killer."

"I like it!" cries Bleak. If he had hands to clap, he would have clapped them. "That Giant's as good as dead."

Chapter Thirteen

THE GIANT IS SITTING on a mountain with his great head in his hands. He is getting hungry now, and tired. And worse: he's starting to feel a little lonely.

Around him as far as even he can see is nothing but ice. Nobody to talk to. Nobody to stroke his hair and whisper a lullaby in his ear. Nobody to tuck him into a huge bed, and no bed to be tucked into, either. His vast heart aches in his chest.

He looks at the mountain beside him, and

he notices that it looks a little like a friend. If he squints, there's a crevasse that looks like a smiling mouth, there's a nose-ish cliff to it. The glacier on top could be hair.

"Oh, hello," he says, pretending that he hadn't noticed his old friend beside him. "You've been here all along. Are you tired?"

He pauses, listening, then brightens.

"Me too! Should we have a nap?"

The mountain apparently thinks this is a good idea. The Giant pets it on its head, and then curls up next to it, cooing. He hums a soft little tune to it, and together they look up at the sky.

"The sky is so big, isn't it?" says the Giant. "It's beautiful, all those stars, so far away. I think they're watching over us. I think we're never really alone, with all those stars up in the sky."

The Giant is lying. In fact, the hugeness of the heavens makes him feel tiny and insignificant. The stars don't care. They were here before

The mountain says nothing.

him and they'll be here when he's gone, always the same, always a million miles away. They will never come down here and give him the nice cup of hot chocolate that he craves. For a moment, his eyes grow teary, but his tears freeze on his eyelids into icebergs. He brushes them away, and sighs.

"You're my best friend in the world," he says to the mountain. The mountain says nothing.

Chapter Fourteen

A S SOON AS THE SHIP HEAVES into view of the Siberian coastline, they can see what horrors have been wrought. The port village they aim to reach is a shambles: some small buildings still standing along the former outskirts, but from the ship's deck our heroes can plainly see the shape of a huge footprint made out of smashed bricks and broken furniture.

What misery, born of the Giant's ignorant foot! People huddle for warmth around fires piled high with wrecked chairs and pianos and beds. Some are vainly trying to reconstruct makeshift shelters against the cold. All are wrapped in blankets and toques and furs so that they look like a gathering of refugee laundry.

Stoat holds Bleak above his head so he can shout clearly as the ship drifts towards the docks. "Do not fret, landlubbers! Bleak the Giant Killer be here!"

But Jack is already astride the Golden Hen, and in a flutter of feathers he is aloft. The graceful leaping chicken hovers flapping for a moment, and then lands on the dock. People scatter every which way.

"Suffering Siberians! It is I, Jack the Famous Giant Killer! You have been plagued, poor people of this village, by enormousness. You have been done injustice by the large. But I have struck down many a mighty foe, yes, I have made them fall down and die. I have killed Giants. That is why they call me Jack the Giant Killer."

CHAPTER FOURTEEN

Everybody looks a little more depressed than he would have hoped. He remembers the glory days, when he would parade through a town like this one and the people would cheer and throw flowers, pretty girls would bat their eyelashes at him; he would stand tall in his stirrups and wave, winking at the girls, and their fathers would be proud that Jack the Giant Killer had winked at their daughters.

But of course these people are looking at a shriveled old man on a chicken. Their hopes are not raised when the ship pulls in and they see the rest of the Giant Killer's entourage—the glowering lady, the fierce tuber, the top-hatted boulder, and the crew of thugs and killers that skitter like wharf rats down the gangway to peer evilly at the townsfolk.

Jack tries again. He rattles his sword heroically. "I will avenge you, people of this town! I will kill the Giant!"

And then he notices, standing not far from

his stirrup, a woman clad all in white fur. He looks closer, and his heart leaps—indeed, the princess is as beautiful as he had hoped. She raises her lovely face to look at him, and bats her long eyelashes. A whisper of a smile passes over her lips, and Jack feels his blood rush within him, filling him with strength like he was thirty years younger. He winks at the princess, and then turns to the crowd again, feeling her gaze hot on his cheek.

"Which way did he go?" Jack shouts, impressively.

A large red-faced man steps forward. The man is also clad in fur, and wears a crown. He is clearly the king of this battered place, and Jack can see the pain of the people's suffering in his eyes. "He went East," he says.

"Then East is my direction," says Jack, peering out the corner of his eye at the princess. She looks back at him, and he grins nobly and raises his arm for a brave salute, when he realizes

CHAPTER FOURTEEN

Amelia is standing next to him with a fierce glint in her eyes.

Jack manages to turn his salute in mid-air into a sweeping gesture towards Amelia. "Ah, my trusted companion," he manages. Amelia glares at him.

Like many men, Jack thinks that what counts is what he does, not what he thinks. And of course, Amelia sees all too well what Jack is thinking, and she is not placated by his last-minute show of loyalty to her, even though Jack, at that moment, is secretly wiping his brow and thinking that he has gotten away with it clean—wondering, even, why Amelia is glaring at him, so completely convinced is he that he is blameless in deed.

"I'll be off, then," says Jack. "Won't be long. See you soon."

But Amelia, grunting, clambers onto the Golden Hen behind him. Jack's shriveled face turns red with annoyance, looking like a beet left too long in a cupboard. He chances a peek at the Siberian princess, and sees her lovely eyes of smoke turn away, and then widen in horror. For the spuming Bleak has arrived.

"Arr!" he gurgles, his beard bristling like a hungry animal lashed to his jaw. His black eyes dart manically. "Simmer down, Princess, old Bleak'll slay yer Giant. Which way did 'e go?"

"East," repeats the king, tired of everybody leering at his daughter.

"East!" cries Jack, wheeling his steed, and surging forward in a lurch of clucking and feathers.

Chapter Fifteen

AND SO THE RAGGED CREW sets forth on the Giant's trail with a wheelchair creak and the rasp of scaly feet on the ice, four intrepid souls alone with their thoughts in the bleak arctic wastes. Not one of them thinks of the Giant they are here to kill.

Bleak's head is a tempestuous squall, raging with visions of stolen glory. The spectres of his lost limbs flex and strain at the miserable wheelchair while his brain twitches, riches and princesses and adulation swimming before him like great fish in a storm-tossed sea.

Jack glowers, plotting the riddance of his wife, the almost-smile of the princess hot in his mind, the cold breath of last-chances in the pit of his stomach.

Amelia's mind is like an iceberg, implacable, victorious. The princess is behind them. But in her guts the Sorcerer asks her why she holds on so tightly to the withered creature before her in the saddle.

Stoat's mind is a placid pond. He thinks of nothing but the trudge.

Not far away now, the Giant is trying to remember what it was like before he was frozen in the iceberg. He can't. He thinks it was less lonely.

Jack is fourteen. He is leading an ancient cow down a dirt road. He watches his feet smacking the beaten brown ground, his toes so filthy they look like stumpy roots. The cow clumps beside him, her bell clanging muffled with an off-beat sway, her spine like a mountain ridge through her thin hair, her nose wet with drool. Jack's shin itches, and he reaches down to scratch it, hopping on one foot with his hand slung through the rope around the plodding cow's neck.

"A splendid beast," says a voice like a wind-rattled window pane.

The cow stops. Jack looks up, his hand still on his shin, his arm outstretched for balance. A man stands before him, a smiling man in a black travelling cloak. His face is soft and friendly. "A splendid beast, I say," says the man, reaching out and stroking the cow's cheek.

Jack observes him dumbly, and finishes scratching. Slowly, he puts his leg down. He has cultivated the appearance of simple-minded hostility for safety's sake. This man might be a bandit, or a priest. Best be silent.

"I'll buy her," says the man, his long finger tracing the cow's ear. The cow stands there as stupidly as Jack.

"What'll I give you for her?" asks the man on sullen Jack's behalf. "Why, I'll give you these beans, boy." The man's hand outstretched, fist closed.

Jack blinks.

"I know what you're thinking," says the man. "You're thinking: Beans?"

Jack looks at the hand.

"No ordinary beans, my boy. These are magic beans—these beans are a gateway to a life of glory. Right now, you are an urchin with a dying cow. That is all. But these beans will give you a name the whole world will know."

Jack looks at the man's face. The man smiles, and opens his hand. In the smooth palm lay three beans. "I might be lying. I might be giving you a handful of ordinary beans. But you'll always wonder—as you grow old and

"You are an urchin with a dying cow. That is all."

grizzled, and finally lie on your deathbed completely forgotten by the world—you'll always
wonder if maybe I wasn't lying. If maybe you
missed your single chance."

Jack takes the beans, and hands the man
the rope. He really has no other choice.

"Plant them, by the way," says the man.
"Don't eat them."

Chapter Sixteen

THE LITTLE INTREPID BAND has decided to stop for the night. They have unfurled their sleeping bags and tents and built a fire. In the vast arctic night their fire looks like a single candle burning in a dark cathedral, four tiny pilgrims gathered to worship, except that their huddled devotions are not holy.

"Cold business, this Giant-hunting," says Bleak, breaking the sullen silence between them. He has frosted right over, and the spokes of his wheelchair are surmounted by snowdrift.

Nobody answers. Stoat moans quietly to himself with his hat pulled down over his blue ears. And Jack is burrowed in his fur sleeping bag, his pale nose protruding to spout thin streams of steam, which entwine in his mind to form a phantasmal Siberian princess. He sighs as he drifts towards the doldrum ripples of sleep.

But where is Amelia? She has wandered off. She is standing outside of the glowing circle, her neck craned to see the stars. In the blackness it feels as if she is floating amongst them. It feels good to breathe the sharp air; it quiets the Sorcerer inside. She feels the glimmer of what it is like to be alive.

Jack, too, is now afloat; he is dreaming of the princess. She is vast and wispy like a cloud, and Jack is gently bobbing in the soft air, carried by eddying currents of breeze towards her. In dreams hearts can ache like a newborn's, and his is pierced with longing, until he is subsumed in the mist. He feels young, like he is at the beginning of a life not yet worn out. There is a castle in the clouds. A sweet voice sings: *Feeeeee*. Jack listens, smiling. *Fiiiiiii*. *Foooooooo*. Jack laughs. *Fuuuuuuuum*. It is a wonderful dream.

Far away the Giant spies the candle flicker in the void, and wonders at it. He squints. In the daytime such a tiny thing would not catch his notice, but from the nighted heavens it is a star out of place, and he decides to investigate. Even for something as huge as the Giant, it beckons warmly.

Suddenly Jack awakes. A strange feeling has crept over him, a nagging thought has interrupted his dream. He furrows his brow in his sleeping bag, thinking. What is it? Something somebody said? Something he's forgotten? Something he's missed?

And then it dawns on him. Bleak wants to kill Giants. Bleak wants to be the Giant Killer. So why did Bleak come and get him?

Jack is sitting up. And there, by the

flickering firelight, he understands. Stoat is digging through Jack's saddle bags in the snow, tossing underwear over his shoulder. Bleak is huffing like a coal-stack, anxiously directing Stoat's searches. He is wearing Jack's Helmet of Knowledge. On his lap lie the Boots of Swiftness.

"Hurry up, Stoat," he hears Bleak whisper. "The Cape, the Sword! Then the Hen!"

Stoat yanks the Cape from the bag with a muffled groan of happiness. Jack grimaces, trying to be quiet. They don't see his Sword, stuck in a snowdrift for quick access in case of Giant attack. He struggles to extricate himself from his sleeping bag, hoping the wind will cover the sound of the zipper. He is half-out and flopping along the ground towards his Sword when Stoat hears him.

"Auwoog," cries Stoat.

"He's awake! Kill him!" cries Bleak. "No wait! Use the Cape of Invisibility!"

CHAPTER SIXTEEN

Stoat is trying to figure out where he puts his head in the Cape, and Jack gets his fingers on the Sword. He tries to stand up but topples, still entangled in the cursed sleeping bag. Stoat has got the Cape inside out.

"Forget the Cape!" barks Bleak, as Jack manages to get one leg out.

There is a rumble of powerful thunder in the distance. The combatants pause.

Bleak's eyes flick to the clear sky, wondering what clouds might gather. But Jack knows the sound of a Giant's footstep.

The Giant's second footfall throws all of them to the ground. Bleak begins to shriek.

The third stride brings the Giant hunched before the fire, and the huddled three find themselves agape before a vast eyeball. Jack frantically tries to free his other leg. Stoat stands paralyzed, staring at himself in the eye like a reflection in a lake. Bleak won't stop screaming.

The eye blinks with a deafening thud. The pupil swivels. A gust blows howling from the far-away nose. A huge finger appears.

"Aaaarrrrgggghhhh-aaaagggg-yeeeer-rrrrgggg!" says Bleak.

Jack is finally out of the sleeping bag. He gets a good grip on his Sword, and prepares to swing.

Out of the corner of his eye he sees Amelia, who is standing with her arms outstretched, her face bright with an ecstatic smile. The gale of the Giant's breath swirls the snow around her, whirling her grey hair; she is a dazzled tornado.

And the fingers pluck her from the earth. A huge shadow passes over the three men as the Giant's foot moves above. The ground shakes, again, again, and the Giant strides away.

Bleak finally stops screaming. Stoat stands dazed. Amelia is gone.

Jack leaps upon the Golden Hen, and with a cluck they are aloft, speeding after the Giant.

Chapter Seventeen

AMELIA SITS LIKE A BEAN in the Giant's outstretched palm. The Giant smiles at her. "Oochy coochy coo," he says. "Coochy oochy coo coo roo. Fee fi fo fum."

"What are you going to do with me?" Amelia asks, trembling, maybe from fear, maybe from wonder.

The Giant grins, uncomprehending. He is clearly fascinated by the creature in his palm, but Amelia thinks he might not realize she is trying to speak. She cups her hands to her mouth and tries again, shouting: "What are you going to do with me?"

The Giant is startled. "I'm sorry, did you just speak?" he says.

Amelia bellows. "Yes, I did. What are you going to do with me?"

"Good lord, I had no idea. I thought you were squeaking or something. How wonderful! You can talk! Can you think and feel as well, or are you just repeating things you've heard?"

The situation dawns on Amelia. The Giant has plucked her from the earth like she would have plucked a ladybug. He thought she was an interesting insect. "Of course I can think and feel," she says, crossing her arms. It occurs to her as she says it that perhaps every ladybug she has ever flicked from her sleeve might have been trying to say something. Or worse: that she is about as smart as a ladybug, compared to the Giant.

The Giant, for his part, is absolutely enthralled. "Do you have a name?' he asks, delighted.

"Amelia," says Amelia. "Do you?"

"I'm sure I do," says the Giant, "but to be honest, I can't remember it. I'm very pleased to meet you, Amelia. What on Earth is it like to be so small?"

"That's a hard question," she says. "I could ask, what on Earth is it like to be so big?"

The Giant laughs, turning his head considerately so that Amelia is not blown away by his breath. He turns back to her when he is done, his face merry and red. "I suppose you are right. Still, we could try to tell each other. Unless—" the Giant stops, his brow crumpling, "Oh no! Have I completely interrupted your evening?"

Amelia does not know quite what to say. "No, no, don't worry," she says.

"Really? I'd be mortified."

"Really. This is altogether fascinating, isn't it?"

"Yes, it is," says the Giant, nodding enthusiastically. "Tell me, are there others like you, or are you a singular miracle?"

Chapter Eighteen

JACK CLUTCHES THE REINS of the Golden Hen with white knuckles under his cold gauntlets. He wheezes as the Hen surges under the saddle, his bony shoulders creaking. They hurtle through the air, land and leap again, the Giant's distant throbbing heart their goal.

He remembers how he found the last Giant he ever saw.

"So you're Jack the Giant Killer," the Giant had said, his great frail body laid out before him, skinny like the frame of a ship draped in

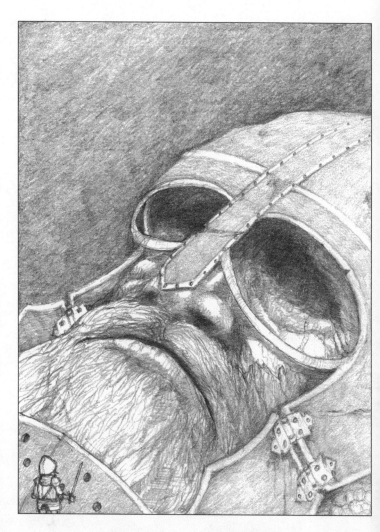

"So you're Jack the Giant Killer."

wet canvas. The Giant breathed hoarsely as he fiddled with his moustache distractedly, his eyes hollow. A pair of vultures hopped along the bony ridge of his outsplayed arm. Jack stood quietly before the vast expiring carcass of the last and oldest of the Giants.

"I've heard a lot about you, of course," said the ancient hulk. "You're a bit late for me, I should say. It won't be long for poor old Pantagruel. I've led a good life, to be sure, but I'm ever so tired now, and I won't be too sad to breathe my last."

Jack looked at his Sword.

"The main thing, I suppose, that gives me pleasure in my last moments," croaked the dying Giant, "is that at least I managed to hide from you long enough to rob you of your final victory. The truth is I probably would have died a while ago if it weren't for you. I've been hold-ing on with all my remaining withered will, just so I could see the look on your face as I died, before you had a chance to stick me with that sword of yours. I won't die because you killed me, you see. I'll die simply of old age. You won't get to slay the Last Giant. It makes me chuckle, a bit."

Jack half-heartedly raised his weapon, but he knew it was fruitless.

"Whoops, there we are then," said the last Giant; and then he breathed his last breath, and his ancient heart stopped beating.

Chapter Nineteen

"MY FAVOURITE THING is walking at night with my head above the clouds. The moon on the back of my neck, cool and blue, the mists stretched before me like ... like an old Giant's beard floating in the tub. I can open my mouth and breathe and drink at the same time because that world is half sea and half wind. Above me, the unhindered light of the stars, and the endless heavens. I like to wonder what it would be like if I could be taller, and stand with my head between the stars, the moon flying by my ear so I have to duck, how wondrous that would be. On nights like those, I never want to sit down, to go back to the shadowy world beneath the clouds, where things are so often grey. When I stand, the world is always clear and perfect, no haze, no confusion. But then I can't bear the beauty, and I have to sit down just to rest my soul. That's what it's like to be me. What's it like to be you?"

Amelia feels a sharp pain in her chest. It is partly envy, and partly regret, and partly shame, and partly a desperate love of life that she feels she has forgotten. It is the forgetting that causes the pain. "It's not like that for me," she says, but then she thinks maybe it is. Some nights are cloudless, after all, but all too often she has chosen to linger under a roof. When she thinks of her life, she cannot recall any part that was roofless. There must have been some, but she can't recall.

CHAPTER NINETEEN

"I'm small enough to get inside of things," she says. "Under blankets, into bedrooms, kitchens. Warm places. I love those things." It's true, she does love them.

"Oh! I see," says the Giant. "That sounds wonderful."

As he says it, she thinks it isn't wonderful at all. She thinks it's the Sorcerer who likes small places, not her. She thinks she's wasted her life. She should have spent it all on top of mountains and towers, as high up as she could be.

But then she sees the Giant's face. His eye is gathering a tear. "A little warm place," he says, "with other little people like yourself, gathered around a fire, chattering and singing with each other, a little world that's exactly the right size for you, no need to be bigger or smaller."

The Giant sighs. "I've never seen anybody else that's my size. Not that I can remember. I might be the only one."

Amelia swallows. She puts her hand on the

Giant's thumb, and strokes it gently. "You are the only one."

The Giant nods. "I thought so," he says, hoarsely.

"Bring me closer," says Amelia. The Giant brings her to his face. She reaches out and hugs his nose. "There, there," she says. "There, there."

And then, out of the corner of her eye, in the distance, she sees Jack coming.

"Run!" cries Amelia. The Giant is startled. "Do as I say! Run!"

Chapter Twenty

JACK'S TEETH ARE CLENCHED, his heels frantically spurring the chicken on. "Faster!" he snarls. The Giant is moving quickly before him, but he too is moving fast, like a revenant arrow, feathers and sharp steel.

"That's my wife, you wretch!" he shouts with all the breath in his old lungs even though the words are carried away by the whistling wind and are behind him even as they come out of his mouth.

The paths to love are many and strange, and sometimes you don't even know you're on one. And grim Jack hurtles onwards.

And grim Jack hurtles onwards.

Chapter Twenty-One

THE GIANT AND AMELIA come to the sea, crashing to a halt at the beleaguered Siberian village. At the docks below, schooners thrash in the waves, and people are running around screaming.

Amelia is on the Giant's head, gripping his tree-trunk hair, scanning the horizon. "I see him!" she cries. "He's coming fast. Keep going!"

The Giant totters at the edge of the water. "No telling how deep it'll get," he says. "It'll slow me down. He'll catch up." He looks back at Jack.

"He's just little," he observes.

"Don't think of fighting him," says Amelia. "He is the bane of your kind. We must keep going."

The Giant has an idea. He leans down and grabs two ships, one in each hand; he shakes them to make sure there's nobody aboard, and then quickly snaps the masts off.

"Hurry!" cries Amelia.

He jams the ships onto his feet, and ties them on with the remaining rigging. He tests one foot in the water; it floats. And the other: it floats too. He takes a few tentative steps into the waves, teetering a little.

"It'll work," he says.

And he strides off over the sea with ships for shoes. Amelia jumps for joy on his head. The Giant laughs.

But they are too late.

Chapter Twenty-Two

WITH A BATTLE-HOWL, Jack flies straight into the Giant's laughing mouth. He banks hard, narrowly missing the tonsils, but the Chicken's momentum hurls them against the back of the esophagus with a shuddering impact. There is a squawking explosion of feathers, and Jack is thrown from the saddle, bouncing off the fleshy wall with a teeth-rattling crunch of armour and brittle bones, finally landing in a heap on the slippery edge of the gizzard tunnel.

He frantically slithers, spinning; a passing glimpse of the dazed Chicken reeling and flapping, and then down, down, in a cascade of drool, into the pitch darkness of the Giant's guts.

Finally he lands with a jarring thump. He lays there stunned, his vision blurry. Far above him there is a light that seems to him a red sun, but it is snowing somehow. He shakes his head and moans. Everything hurts. Slowly he realizes that the sun is the soft gleam of sunlight in the mouth far above, and the snowfall is feathers floating languidly down.

His fingers twitch. There; he still grasps his Sword. Clenching his jaw, Jack manages to sit up. Beyond the faint glimmer from above, he is in total darkness. He guesses he is in the stomach.

He creaks to his feet, and straightens his breastplate. He sheathes CloudSlicer, for he has some climbing to do. He will make his way, viruslike, to the heart.

Chapter Twenty-Three

"Swallow me," says Amelia to the Giant.

"But I'll digest you!" the Giant protests.

"It must be done. Swallow me, and then spit me up later. I have to stop Jack."

"How will I know to spit you up? How will I know you've stopped him?"

"If you're still alive."

The Giant regards the tiny, fierce old woman in his hand, his brow furrowed with worry.

"Hurry! Even now he is making his way to your heart!"

The Giant raises her to his mouth. "Little person," he says, "be careful in there. It will be dark and dangerous."

"I know," says Amelia, determined.

"You're my only friend," says the Giant.

"You're my only friend, too," says Amelia. "Whatever happens down there, at least we know that much."

The Giant nods, a sad smile on his face.

"Do you like the name 'Edward?'" says Amelia.

"I think so," says the Giant.

"I'll call you Edward."

Then the Giant opens his mouth, and gently puts Amelia in. He can hear her shout from inside himself: "Swallow, Edward, swallow!"

And he does.

Chapter Twenty-Four

JACK IS HALFWAY UP the Giant's gullet. He can make out the passage to the heart in the faint red glimmer, not far above him. His stringy muscles ache, and his breathing is hoarse and laboured. His fingers are lanced with pain, clutching the spongy wall of the esophagus, heaving his battered ancient body upward. His legs shake with exertion. He is far too old for this; the effort is more than his body can bear. The croaking voice of Death whispers in his ear. But upwards he climbs nonetheless—for this Giant has stolen his wife. He has one more Giant to kill before he dies, and one more princess to save.

The Giant is speaking, he thinks. He is buffeted by the roiling winds of his breath, and he can hear the vast thrum of the vocal chords vibrating, like a symphony of bass cellos. He cannot make out the words. Jack trembles, hanging onto a handhold, resting for a brief moment to gather his strength. One more heave and he will be there.

And then the great glottis moves. Jack can barely hold on. The Giant is swallowing. Jack whimpers with strain, buffeted by a waterfall of drool, the heaving of the very wall he grips. He feels his fingers begin to slip.

Then the throat is still. He almost weeps with relief, but he must go on. He raises his hand to try for a higher purchase.

He is there, grunting as he hoists his old

self onto the lip of the tunnel. He lies there, panting.

And he does not see Amelia hurtle past the mouth of his cave, her eyes wide. She sees him, however, as she plummets down the great wet chimney to land in a heap far below.

Chapter Twenty-Five

Jack struggles to his feet, dizzy with exhaustion, and draws his sword. Into the tunnel he goes.

The vascular passage is a maze of twists and turns and forking paths, but Jack knows the insides of Giants well. He presses his ear against the wall and listens for the rumbling drum rhythm of the heart. He is gaining strength; this is familiar ground. He navigates the labyrinth like the resident minotaur.

And finally he is there, standing in the vaulted chamber of the heart. It booms with each beat, huge coiling vessels pulsing with the throb of lifeblood flowing. He raises CloudSlicer with a sure fist.

He pauses for a moment. This heart is the heart of his own life, he feels; this will be his last gesture in this world. He has savoured much glory in his time, yes; he has reaped the benefits of fame and wealth. He has saved princesses, so many he cannot remember their faces anymore. He has heard his name from so many lips: Jack the Giant Killer! And he has always hungered to hear it again, again, again.

But that is not what he hears at that moment. What he hears is so much less, and yet so much more. It is simply *Jack*.

He turns when he hears his name. Amelia is behind him.

"You're alive!" he cries. He is flooded with joy and relief that is strange to him. Before he knows it, he is hugging her. It is right, he thinks: this is the first princess he ever saved, and now the last—all his life she has truly been the only princess. Forget the white furs and the red lips! How sweet this grizzled wife of his, how familiar those pale and shriveled lips! How that wrinkled cheek fits his own! How good to hear his name from that familiar throat!

"I am here, dear wife! I shall save you from this Giant, like I did so many years ago! Another chance!" He holds her before him, grinning, and only slowly does it dawn on him that there is no gratitude in her eyes.

Liar, whispers the Sorcerer. Amelia blinks in Jack's arms. The Sorcerer had been quiet for some time. She listens to him. *All he wants is another princess.* She does not hug Jack back.

Jack recoils, stung. "Well, then. Stand back. I am the Giant Killer. I have business. It will be gruesome." He turns, the back of his neck burning, and raises his sword.

"Stand back. I am the Giant Killer."

CHAPTER TWENTY-FIVE

"Don't kill the Giant," says Amelia.

"What?" Jack is annoyed now.

"I said don't kill the Giant."

"Absurd," says Jack. "I am Jack the Giant Killer. It's what I do."

"I'll tell you what I think, Jack. I'll tell you what I've decided. I've decided I don't care if you're the Giant Killer or not. It's never done me any good. I've never loved you. What's more, you've never loved me. This Giant loves me. This Giant who doesn't even know his own name, who wants nothing but love and the sky. A much better creature than you, Jack. I love him, not you."

Jack's sword drops. He feels terribly old. Here in the hot centre of the Giant, he feels a cold wind. "I'm Jack the Giant Killer," he mumbles. "Jack the Giant Killer. Princesses love *me*, not Giants. I kill Giants." With a creak of dry bones, he crumples to the floor.

Ordinary beans, he thinks. They were ordinary beans. Just a pathetic bean sprout in the backyard, his mother weeping in the kitchen. Jack sitting in a dirty shirt with his head in his hands, staring out the glass-less window, dreaming of glory and feeling small. Imagining princesses. One morning, his mother finding him standing on the beanstalk, the scrawny thing crushed under his filthy toes, swinging a stick. His eyes glazed. Finally, leaving, never to return to that grubby hovel.

The Giant's great heart booms. Jack stares blankly at his hand. "Get up, old man," says Amelia. "We're leaving this place."

But Jack is a muttering heap. He can't feel his legs; they are nothing but strange twigs. His arms are numb. A horrible stillness is creeping over him. He cannot move. CloudSlicer slithers from his insensate fingers.

Amelia takes the Sword and thrusts it through her belt. She grabs him under his armpits, and heaves him onto her shoulders.

CHAPTER TWENTY-FIVE

He is as light as ink on paper.

She carries him down the passage from the Giant's heart. He moans quietly on her back. In his dimming vision he sees the great heart recede, as his own heart too grows smaller and smaller.

Chapter Twenty-Six

THE GIANT BALANCES UNCERTAINLY on the gently rocking sea, poised, trying to understand what is transpiring inside himself. It feels odd in his chest, he thinks, although he's not sure; maybe he can feel feet treading in his veins, or maybe veins always feel this way, but he's never noticed. He tries to still his breathing, to keep his innards safe for Amelia's mission. Seagulls circle his legs, thinking they have found a new island to lay eggs and poop upon.

The Giant hears something. He concentrates: it is a voice, he thinks. His ears strain with effort.

"Spit us up," he thinks it says. He brightens. It is the voice of Amelia, he's sure of it. With great joy, he opens his mouth wide, and spits into his hand.

A muddled thing lands in his palm, two tiny sets of arms and legs scrambled together like a hairball.

"Amelia!" he cries. Amelia disentangles herself from the unmoving pile of Jack, and grins back at the Giant.

"You're safe," says Amelia, beaming. She hugs the Giant's thumb, and the Giant sheds a great tear.

"You're safe," says the Giant. "That's what matters to me. I don't know what I would have done if I had digested you."

Jack moans softly. The Giant peers at him.

"This must be Jack," he says.

CHAPTER TWENTY-SIX

"It is," says Amelia. "My husband. Jack the Giant Killer."

"Jack," whispers Jack. "Jack the Giant Killer. Jack the Princess Saver. Jack the Chicken Rider. Jack the Memoir Writer. Jack the . . . Jack the . . ." He peters out.

"He looks very sad," says the Giant.

Jack hears it as though underwater. He feels a dark tide coming over his mind, lapping, lapping, and he tries to remember his name. He is half-relieved when he realizes he can't.

Amelia cannot be quite as hardened as she planned. Something makes her kneel beside him.

Jack's vision is dimming when he sees a flicker of movement through the fog. Something dark and bristling on the Giant's earlobe. Something vicious; something hairy. Something bellowing.

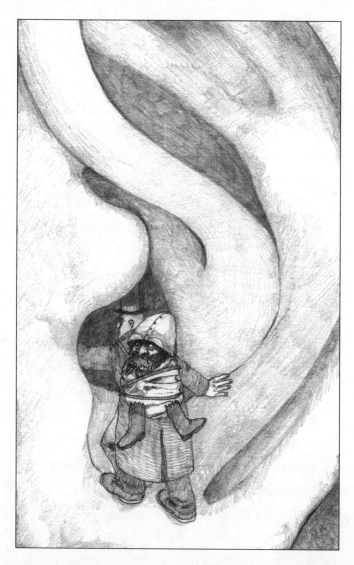

"Bleak the Giant Killer! Bleak! Bleak the Giant Killer!"

Chapter Twenty-Seven

"BLEAK THE GIANT KILLER!" shrieks Bleak from the Giant's ear. "Bleak the Giant Killer! Bleak! Bleak the Giant Killer!"

He is tied to the rockface back of Stoat, wriggling like a vile larva in a papoose. On his head is the Helmet, and he is wrapped in the Cape. The Boots are crudely sewn onto his bum. Stoat clings patiently, waiting for Bleak's victory froth to finish. With one hand he holds onto the ear, with the other he holds a sinister black harpoon.

"I know everything! I'm fast fast fast! Can't see me, can't see me, Cape of In-vis-ibility!"

Everybody can see Bleak.

"Into the ear, into the ear, into the ear, kill the Giant! Whoopee!" Bleak sings weirdly.

"What's happening?" cries the Giant.

"Oh no! Oh no!" cries Amelia.

"Princess! Mine! Princess! Mine!" foams Bleak.

And then: a shrill whistle. Amelia turns; in slowed time she sees Jack sitting up, his face contorted with effort, still whistling.

From the Giant's nostril hurtles the Golden Hen, answering her master's call. Her wings flap furiously, and in a graceful arc she sweeps down from the nose to the Giant's palm, Jack's hand outstretched, grabbing the reins, the Chicken's momentum flinging him up and over and onto the saddle, a flurry of wingbeats and they are airborne, Jack wrenching the reins into a tight bank towards the Giant's ear.

Bleak's eyes widen. It is all happening too fast. "Stoat!" he cries, and Stoat swivels just in time to feel the impact of the charging Chicken. The whole gangle of whalers and feathers and Jack tumble into the Giant's ear with a howl and a crash.

Jack staggers to his feet, breathing hard, and fumbles for the Sword that isn't in its sheath. He shakes his head to clear the fog. His arms hurt. His knees shake. Across the eardrum he sees Stoat stagger also to his feet, the fearsome worm Bleak unslung and writhing on the ground between them.

Jack flexes his empty fingers. Stoat hefts his harpoon from hand to hand. They circle, feeling the ground under their feet like a flesh trampoline. Each step they take reverberates like a huge drumbeat.

Jack sees the glimmer of attack in Stoat's eyes. The charge is about to come. The harpoon is like an iron shadow between them.

"How'd ye see me?" gurgles Bleak.

"Now you know the truth," says Jack, watching the stalking Stoat. "Just a cape, really. The helmet is hot and uncomfortable, that's all. And the boots are nothing but out of fashion. Being the Giant Killer really isn't as rewarding as you might think."

"I'm the Giant Killer! Me!" Bleak slobbers.

Jack moves quickly. He leaps into the air with all his remaining might. Stoat swivels his muscled shoulders to throw the harpoon, his tiny marble eyes following Jack through the air, up, up, and then down, to land beside Bleak upon the taut drumhead floor. And Bleak bounces like an angry ball into the air, propelled by Jack's impact.

For a strange moment, Jack and Stoat watch as Bleak hovers in the air between them.

And then nimble old Jack snatches the screaming lump from the air. He clutches the creature to his chest and runs, Stoat following making a terrifying high-pitched moan. To the earlobe he leaps, and lifts the thrashing Bleak above his head. He turns and faces Stoat, who is poised to throw the harpoon.

Jack looks into Stoat's eyes, his belly exposed. Stoat looks back.

"This Giant," pants Jack, "will live."

Stoat pauses, the harpoon trembling in his meaty hand.

"Death to the Giant!" screeches Bleak.

An understanding passes between the old man and the huge whaler. Stoat's pebble eyes soften. He nods, and lowers his harpoon.

Jack turns and hurls the hairy wad from the Giant's ear. It takes a terribly long time for the thing to fall. Stoat and Jack watch it go.

Far below them, there is a tiny splash.

They look at each other, and smile.

Bleak sinks like a cannonball into the depthless sea, desperately holding his breath. As the sea grows darker and darker, he sees with horror the gathering of the cod. The last darkness for Bleak is the darkness of the Cod King's gullet.

"A gift from the New God! A miraculous gift!" cry the cod.

Chapter Twenty-Eight

AMELIA PUTS HER ARMS around Jack with tears in her eyes. The Sorcerer slithers out of her, never to return.

"Jack," she says. "The Saviour of the Last Giant."

"No, no," he says. "Jack will do."

They turn and wave to Stoat, who waves back from his far-away boat at the Giant's feet, holding a huge gold egg in his other hand; a gift from the Golden Hen. Stoat sets sail into the wide ocean.

The Giant speaks. "Thank you, Jack."

Jack looks up at his huge face. "My wife and I have a house that's big enough for three."

Amelia nods.

The Giant smiles. "That would be wonderful," he says.

"Good," says Jack. "Let's go, then."

And so the three head home, and so ends the story.

And so too end the memoirs of Jack, known as the Giant Killer, for there were no more deeds to do. All that could be done was done, and that was the end of it.

THE END

003453